The King's Secret

THE LEGEND OF KING SEJONG

Carol Farley

Illustrated by

Robert Jew

HarperCollinsPublishers

The King's Secret

Text copyright © 2001 by Carol Farley

Illustrations copyright © 2001 by Robert Jew

Printed in the U.S.A. All rights reserved. www.harperchildrens.com

Library of Congress Cataloging-in-Publication Data

Farley, Carol J.

   The king's secret / Carol Farley ; illustrated by Robert Jew.

      p.   cm.

   Summary: With the help of a scholar and a young gardener, the wise king of Korea introduces an alphabet that will enable his people to read and write in their own language. Based on Korean legends.

   ISBN 0-688-12776-2 — ISBN 0-688-12777-0 (lib. bdg.)

   1. Sejong, King of Korea, 1397–1450—Juvenile fiction.   [1. Sejong, King of Korea, 1397–1450—Fiction.

2. Korean language—Alphabet—Fiction.   3. Korea—History—Fiction.]   I. Jew, Robert, ill.   II. Title.

PZ7.F233 Ki   2001   00-046101

[Fic]—dc21

Typography by Matt Adamec   1 2 3 4 5 6 7 8 9 10   ❖   First Edition

This book is dedicated to
Kaitlin Farley Crean,
Gordon Thomas Crean,
Paul Ryan Duran,
Christopher Jordan Duran,
Nicholas Alan Duran,
Roxanne Geneva Farley,
George Roger Farley,
and Owen Douglas Mitchell,
because, like Yong Tu,
they know the joy of reading.
—C. F.

This book is dedicated to my wife,
Kitty, for her love and support,
and my son, Maxson,
for his hugs and kisses.
—R. J.

Long ago, when tigers smoked long pipes and rabbits talked to dragons, a rich king ruled the land of Korea. The sun itself did not shine as brilliantly as the gold gleaming in his magnificent throne. The stars in the midnight sky did not glitter as brightly as the jewels on his splendid robes. The pieces of jade in his money box were as plentiful as the leaves on the trees in the gardens surrounding his enormous palace.

King Sejong was wise as well as wealthy. "All of this is very good," he often said as he looked at his possessions, "but my greatest treasure is in my mind. Because I can read and write, I am a rich man indeed."

At the far end of one of the many garden paths, the son of one of King Sejong's kitchen servants worked from dawn till dusk. Yong Tu tended all the flowers and bushes and trees near a beautiful lotus pool. He, too, was wise. But he had no riches, for he had no possessions and he could neither read nor write.

One day King Sejong was walking down this garden path. He had left behind his jewels and his robe with its embroidered dragon. "I wish to truly know my people," he had told his friend Chong In-ji that morning. "If they know that I am their king, they are too frightened to speak. If I dress like an ordinary man, they will talk more freely, and I will know their thoughts."

Soon he reached the pool, and as he stopped there to admire the lotus flowers, he saw Yong Tu drawing a stick across the dirt. "Are you doing your lessons?" he asked.

If Yong Tu had known that the man who spoke was the great King Sejong, he would have fallen flat to the earth in humility and awe. But he thought this man was one of the many scholars who visited the palace. And so he politely gave the deep bow that shows respect for someone older and wiser. "No, honored sir, I am not."

"Are you lazy, then?" the king asked. "Would you rather play games than read and write?"

Yong Tu stood up straighter. "All of my life I have wanted to read and write!"

King Sejong liked the way the boy's eyes sparkled. "Then why don't you begin your studies?"

"Because I don't have the money to pay a teacher." Yong Tu's shoulders drooped. "And I don't have much time, either, after my hours of working here in the garden."

"Yes," the king agreed, "it is true that you need great sums of money and many years of study. We may speak Korean, but we read and write only in Chinese. An educated person must know many thousands of Chinese characters."

Yong Tu sighed. "I would give half the years of my life if I could read and write. But I know it is not possible for me to do it in the Chinese way. I wish we had our own Korean way to make written words."

"I have often had that same wish myself," the king answered.

Yong Tu pointed to the flowers floating in the water. "I wish that our writing symbols could be like them—few in number, simple and beautiful."

The words of the small gardener echoed in King Sejong's mind as he continued on his walk. The boy was hardworking and eager to learn. Surely there had to be a way to help him.

Deep in thought, the king wandered down paths hidden among the bushes. Wind rustled and breezes whispered through the leaves of the mulberry trees, mockingbirds called from overhead branches, and crickets chirped from below. Water trickled and rippled from underground springs.

Chinese writing shows the beauty of the language with word pictures, he thought, but nature shows its beauty with sounds as well as sights. Could we show the beauty of the Korean language by finding a way to write its sounds?

The king was still wondering about this as he left the shadows of the trees. In the distance he saw the gentle slopes of the huge mountains that silently guarded his kingdom like a circle of faithful tortoises. They seemed alive, brimming with wisdom. "Is such a thing possible, Mountain Spirit?" he asked. Holding his breath, he listened for an answer.

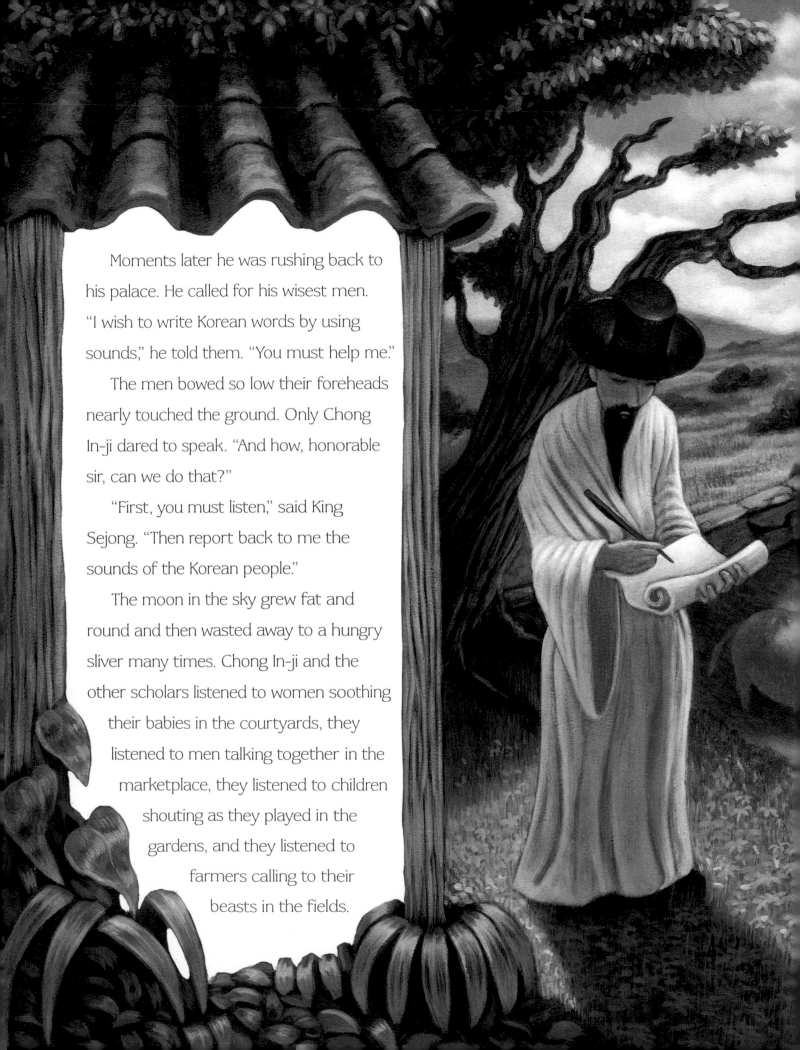

Moments later he was rushing back to his palace. He called for his wisest men. "I wish to write Korean words by using sounds," he told them. "You must help me."

The men bowed so low their foreheads nearly touched the ground. Only Chong In-ji dared to speak. "And how, honorable sir, can we do that?"

"First, you must listen," said King Sejong. "Then report back to me the sounds of the Korean people."

The moon in the sky grew fat and round and then wasted away to a hungry sliver many times. Chong In-ji and the other scholars listened to women soothing their babies in the courtyards, they listened to men talking together in the marketplace, they listened to children shouting as they played in the gardens, and they listened to farmers calling to their beasts in the fields.

At last they felt ready to meet with the king. "There are twenty-eight different sounds," Chong In-ji told him. "When these sounds are put together, all Korean words can be made."

King Sejong smiled. "Good. But our work is not over. We must make a symbol for each sound. When our people learn those twenty-eight symbols, they will be able to read and write every Korean word."

Once again Chong In-ji bowed deeply. "And what kinds of symbols would you like, honorable sir?"

"Look at the world around you," King Sejong said. "Look at mountains and lotus flowers and cherry blossoms and cranes. Look at tigers and clouds and bamboo trees and rivers. Take whatever is beautiful and good and draw it into a symbol that will be one Korean sound."

Many times the moon in the sky grew fat and round and then wasted away to a hungry sliver as the wise men worked. At last they had created twenty-eight symbols. Carefully they painted them on a long banner.

King Sejong rejoiced. The symbols were few in number, and they were simple and beautiful—exactly what Yong Tu had wanted. He could hardly wait to see the boy. By now they had become good friends for, dressed like an ordinary man, the king had visited him often.

"King Sejong has declared that Koreans need their own alphabet," he told Yong Tu later that day as he unfurled the long banner. "Each of these symbols is one sound. Can you learn them all quickly?"

"Of course I can!" Quietly Yong Tu listened to the sound of each. Before the sun had set, he knew all twenty-eight symbols.

"A child has learned this alphabet in just a few hours," the king told the men of his court that evening. "Soon every Korean will be able to read and write!"

But King Sejong was mistaken.

Important people in all the cities and villages looked at the symbols and whispered among themselves. "We cannot use them," they told one another. "King Sejong is great, but the gods are even greater. Koreans have always used the Chinese way of writing, because the gods will it."

Many weeks later Chong In-ji told the king the sad news. "People don't like the new alphabet. They say the gods have blessed only the Chinese way of writing."

"The gods can bless more than one way of writing!" King Sejong declared. "We must think of how to show people this truth."

But no matter how hard he and the scholars of his court tried, they could not think of a way to do this.

Finally King Sejong put on his humble clothing and went back to visit Yong Tu. "I'm sorry," he said, "but Korean words will not be written with the new symbols after all."

Yong Tu caught his breath in amazement. "Why not?"

"Many teachers and village elders say the Chinese characters were a gift from the gods, like the mountains and the tigers and the gardens and the trees. They have always been with us. People say that the gods have given no sign that a new alphabet should be used in our land."

"Sometimes it is hard to know what the gods will." Yong Tu pointed to a small mound of sand surrounded by bits of dead leaves. "Do they will that those ants destroy the beauty of the pathway I have just cleaned?"

King Sejong laughed. "There will always be insects in a garden," he said. And as the words came from his lips, a wonderful idea came into his mind. He jumped to his feet. "Yong Tu! Can you work quickly? King Sejong will be bringing some very important men to this lotus pool tomorrow evening!"

"The king!" Yong Tu dropped to his knees. "The king?"

"Yes." King Sejong pulled the boy to his feet. "Come now, Small Dragon, I'll tell you what you must do."

The sun was slowly sinking behind the mountains as King Sejong led a parade of teachers, village elders, and soldiers along the path the next evening. Shafts of light radiated across the sky, doves cooed, and crickets sang. The sweet fragrance of roses drifted on the pleasant breezes in the dappling twilight.

"I believe the gods themselves are in this garden tonight," King Sejong said, and everyone murmured agreement.

Soon they were near Yong Tu's lotus pool. Suddenly a village elder gasped. He pointed to the leaves of a nearby tree. "But look! What is this? What is this?"

Everyone drew closer to stare at the tree. In the fading twilight, each leaf clearly showed the outline of one of the new Korean writing symbols.

"And look here!" a soldier cried. "Here is another tree exactly like that one!"

The men scurried from tree to tree, from bush to bush, shouting and laughing. On many leaves the symbols of the new alphabet had been etched, as if they had been carved there by the finger of a god.

"This is a miracle!" a teacher declared. "A miracle from heaven! The gods are showing us that we must use the new Korean symbols to write Korean words."

King Sejong nodded. "Yes, I believe the gods will it."

Chong In-ji motioned to the men. "You must go back to your villages and begin writing with the new symbols. You must teach others the new alphabet so that they, too, will be able to read Korean words. The gods have spoken!"

King Sejong stood quietly as they hurried away. Then, smiling, he removed his kingly robe and walked back into the bushes behind the lotus pool where Yong Tu was waiting. "You did well," he told the boy. "You helped the gods speak."

"The insects did most of the work." Yong Tu held up an empty honey jar. "I only wrote the new symbols on the leaves as you told me to do."

King Sejong bent down to look into Yong Tu's eyes. "I think people will be more willing to use our new alphabet now. But you saw the wisdom of our Korean symbols from the very beginning. Come to the palace with me, and soon you'll be reading and writing. Come share your wisdom and knowledge with the king."

"With the king!" Yong Tu gasped. "But, honored sir, can you speak for the great King Sejong himself?"

"Yes," said the king. And then he told the boy his secret.

A Note from the Author

Although some of the people and events in *The King's Secret* were inspired by a Korean legend and my own imagination, much of this story is based on truth.

King Sejong, born in 1397, ruled the peninsula of Korea from 1418 to 1450. Sometimes called the Leonardo of the Orient because he displayed genius in so many areas, King Sejong brought peace, culture, and prosperity to his people. During his reign, astonishing progress was made in astronomical science, music, medicine, and foreign relations. But the most lasting innovation he brought about was the invention of *hangeul*, an entirely new system of writing.

Previous to the use of this phonetic method for communicating sounds and words, all educated Koreans spoke both Korean and Chinese but wrote only in Chinese. A basic knowledge of thirty thousand characters was essential. Since few Koreans had the time and money necessary for years of study, most could neither read nor write.

As a Confucian, King Sejong valued education. He announced that he wished to develop a special alphabet so that Koreans could read and write in their own language. He called on Chong In-ji, who was one of the most respected members in his palace "Hall of Worthies." Together, they and other scholars found that by combining twenty-eight different sounds, every word of the Korean language could be expressed.

Great care was used in creating symbols for these sounds. Each of the seventeen consonants was drawn to show the area of the mouth needed for its pronunciation. The eleven vowels were devised to symbolize heaven, earth, and humanity—all the elements constituting their view of the universe.

In 1446 the alphabet was presented to the public. "A wise person can learn these simple symbols in a few hours," King Sejong is reported to have stated. "And even a foolish person can learn them in ten days." He was pleased that at last all the people in his kingdom would be able to read and write.

Some of Korea's leading educators, who were also its religious leaders, saw this possibility as a threat to their way of life. Choe Malli led an attack against the use of hangeul. He and many other Confucians felt that literacy should be a privilege only the elite enjoyed. Many Koreans still believed in animism, whereby everything in nature had a divine spirit. Their religious leaders, called shamans, acted as intermediaries between these gods and humanity. Some shamans taught that all new ideas were displeasing to the gods.

Although some Buddhist monks recognized the value of hangeul and began using it in their religious writings, others said that the Chinese method was so superior nothing should replace it. Often these religious leaders hid their true feelings by declaring that the gods wished them to continue using only Chinese characters. Legends grew about the ways King Sejong and his supporters tried to convince the general public to accept the new alphabet.

One legend tells how King Sejong invited village elders, government officials, military officers, and other important men to walk in the palace gardens. There they found the new symbols etched into the leaves of trees. The old story says that the king encouraged them to believe that this was the gods' way of blessing the new system of writing. In 1947 Doubleday published one version of the story for English-speaking readers. Frances Carpenter used earthworms instead of insects for her "Letters from Heaven" in *Tales of a Korean Grandmother*. I am indebted to this author for introducing me to this charming legend.

There was no child mentioned in Carpenter's tale, nor in any other version I read, but a boy certainly might have painted the leaves at the king's command. Lowly garden creatures always played the same role that they play in *The King's Secret*.

No record exists that King Sejong disguised himself as an ordinary man, but this behavior is often reported about ancient Korean royalty. In any case, we know that he used every possible means to convince his people that his new alphabet should be adopted.

Over the centuries, the value of hangeul has proved that the king's convictions were correct. Today the alphabet has been reduced to twenty-four letters, and 95 percent of all Koreans are literate. Experts in communication agree that hangeul is one of the world's most logical methods of writing.

Because modern Koreans recognize the debt they owe to the man who inspired this system, King Sejong has been honored in many ways. His image appears on postage stamps and money, and his name identifies boulevards, cultural centers, foundations, and prizes. October 9 has been declared Hangeul Day in Korea. On this holiday schoolchildren visit statues and shrines to show their respect for King Sejong. They call him the greatest monarch of the Yi Dynasty.

Modern Hangeul Symbols

CONSONANTS

Symbol	Sounds like
ㅂ	*b, p*
ㅊ	*ch*
ㄷ	*d, t*
ㄱ	*g, k*
ㅎ	*h*
ㅈ	*ch, j*
ㅋ	*k*
ㅁ	*m*
ㄴ	*n*
ㅇ	Silent before vowel; *ng* in middle or at end of word
ㅍ	*p*
ㄹ	*r, l*
ㅅ	*s*
ㅌ	*t*

VOWELS

Symbol	Sounds like	

These five vowels are written next to the consonants.

Symbol	Sounds like	
ㅏ	*a*	(father)
ㅑ	*ya*	(yacht)
ㅓ	*o*	(onion)
ㅕ	*yo*	(young)
ㅣ	*i*	(marine)

Symbol	Sounds like	

These five vowels are written under the consonants.

Symbol	Sounds like	
ㅗ	*o*	(old)
ㅛ	*yo*	(yodel)
ㅜ	*oo*	(spook)
ㅠ	*yu*	(yule)
ㅡ	*u*	(utter)

JUN 2 4 2002